Why be unfriendly?

By Janine Amos and Annabel Spenceley
Consultant Rachael Underwood

A Cherrytree Book
First published in paperback in 2003
Designed and produced by A S Publishing
Design and typesetting by James Leaman and Michael Leaman

First published 2000
by Cherrytree Press, a division of Evans
Brothers Limited
2A Portman Mansions
Chiltern St
London WIU 6NR
Reprinted 2003

British Library Cataloguing in Publication Data
Amos, Janine
Why be unfriendly?. – (Problem solvers)
1. Friendship – Juvenile literature
2. Social interaction – Juvenile literature
I. Title II. Spenceley, Annabel
302.3'4

ISBN 1 842 34192 8

Printed in Italy by G. Canale & C. S.p.A. - Turin

Why be unfriendly?

Sometimes you and your friends may want to play on your own. But that could be a problem if others want to play too. When you want different things you can learn to work it out together. Here are some steps to help you.

 First of all, let everyone say how they feel

 Say what the problem is

 Talk about different ways to solve the problem

 Then choose a way that makes everyone happy

The children in this book all help each other to solve problems. As you read, see if you can follow the problem-solving steps they use.

The Password

It's morning playtime and everyone rushes into
the playground. Caitlin, Sita and Holly can't wait to get
on with their game.

"Don't forget – we're up to the part where we try to get out of the Magic Maze!" says Holly.

Just then, Holly sees Alice coming over to them.

"Quickly!" Holly tells the others. "Start playing before she comes."

The girls run about, pretending they are lost.

Alice stands and watches them.

"What are you playing?" she asks.

But Caitlin, Sita and Holly don't even look at Alice. They just carry on playing.

"Hey!" says Alice loudly. "Can I play?"
The other girls don't answer her.
"Let's use the Magic Password," says Holly, in the game.
Caitlin, Sita and Holly stand together holding hands. They
turn their backs on Alice and whisper a long word.

Alice is left out. She goes and sits on the bench with her head down. She feels sad.

After a while, Sita goes over to Alice and sits next to her.
"Stop a minute!" says Sita to the others. "Alice is crying!"
They all gather round.
"What's the matter?" asks Holly.

"I want to play!" says Alice.

"You can't," Holly replies. "We started this game yesterday. You don't know it – you were away."

"We could make up a new game," says Sita. "Then Alice can play too."

"No!" say Holly and Caitlin together. "This one's fun."

They all stand and look at Alice. She's thinking.
"Tell me the story," she says, after a while.
"Then I can join in."

"We won't have time." says Caitlin. "Playtime's nearly over already!"

"We can carry on after lunch," says Sita.

They all sit down on the bench. Holly starts to
explain the game to Alice.

"There's even a Magic Password!" Holly tells her.
The four girls hold hands. Then Sita, Caitlin and Holly
whisper the Password to Alice.

Goal shooting

Michel and Tom are playing with a football. They are practising goal-shooting. First Michel is in goal and Tom kicks. After ten kicks they swap over.

Ben comes running up. For a while he stands and watches. Then he shouts, "To me!"

"No! We're practising!" calls Tom.

Ben feels angry. He runs at the ball. He kicks it away from Michel.

"Give it back!" shouts Michel, chasing after the ball.

Ben elbows Michel out of the way. Michel trips as he
tries to reach the ball. Tom runs over and grabs Ben's arm.
"Give that ball back!" shouts Tom.

"Get off!" yells Ben.
They start to pull each other's sweatshirts.

Mrs Casey sees them and hurries over.
"Stop!" she calls. "What's the problem?"
"They won't let me play!" shouts Ben.

The three boys all begin to talk at once.
 "One at a time," says Mrs Casey, "so I can hear."

One by one the boys explain.

"So, you two are practising – and now Ben wants to join you. What could you do?" asks Mrs Casey.

"Let's have a kickaround," suggests Ben. "We can all play that!"

"We want to practise goal-shooting," says Tom.

"Is there any way that three can play goal-shooting?" asks the teacher.
They all think.

Michel comes up with an idea.

"We can take turns," he suggests. "Everyone has a turn at kicking – then at goal-keeping – then at waiting!"

"OK! Ten kicks each, and then change," says Tom.
"OK!" agrees Ben.

"Is everyone happy with that plan?" asks Mrs Casey.
The boys all nod. They run off to try it.

"You've sorted it out!" says Mrs Casey, smiling.

When there's a problem

When you are busy playing with your friends, it's sometimes easy to leave someone out. You don't mean to be unfriendly. You just want to get on with the game. But if someone is being left out, there is a problem.

If you notice someone is left out, stop playing. Talk about it and work out how you can all play. If you are the one being left out, tell the others that you want to join in. Try to solve the problem together. That way, everyone can be happy.

Problem Solving

The children in Mrs Casey's class solved their problems.
They remembered a few problem-solving ideas:

 Let everyone say how they feel

 Share information about what happened
and let everyone say what they want

 Be clear about what the problem is

 Talk about different ideas for sorting out the problem

 Agree on an idea together – and try it out!

This plan might help you next time you have a problem to
solve. Sometimes a problem may seem too big to tackle alone.
You might need to talk about it with an adult first.